HANNE'S QUEST

To (Miss) Patti, who shares the journey...

HANNE'S QUEST

Olivier Dunrea

PHILOMEL BOOKS

Chapter 1

MEM POCKETS RECEIVES A LETTER

ON A SMALL FARM in Moolland, near the village of Skara Bree, there lived a quiet woman whom everyone called Mem Pockets. She was called Mem Pockets because her apron and dress had many pockets that bulged with tasty treats—dog biscuits for her dog friends, kernels of corn for her fowl friends, and dark chocolate for her children friends.

Mem Pockets lived alone, but she was not lonely. Her closest companions were her dog, Daisy, and her small flock of speckled hens—Scaldy hens. Mem Pockets loved Daisy very much. She loved her speckled hens with all her heart. Her Scaldy hens laid the most beautiful eggs in the islands.

Each morning Mem Pockets shared her breakfast of hot, crusty bread and cheese with Daisy. She drank strong coffee with lots of cream. After breakfast Mem Pockets walked to the henwoodie, or henhouse, and fed the hens their morning meal of crushed corn.

"Good morning, my darlings. It is another lovely day," she sang.

The hens clucked excitedly back to her. Mem Pockets chattered and sang to the hens as she tipped their feed into the wooden trough. The hens clustered eagerly around her feet, pecking at the old woman's clogs and scrambling to get into their places for the morning meal. Each hen had her own place at the trough.

Mem Pockets spied the small black hen sitting on the roost.

"Come, Hanne," she said. "Don't you want to eat your breakfast before going out into the farmyard?"

Hanne was the smallest and youngest of the hens. She had not yet begun to lay eggs. Mem Pockets thought she was one of the most beautiful Scaldy hens she had ever seen. Her feathers were midnight black with flecks of tiny white dots scattered over them. Hanne's comb was bright red and stood upright. Her tail feathers were sleek and trim. Hanne never scrambled with the other hens at mealtimes. Mem Pockets nearly always had to coax her to come and get her fair share of the food.

Hanne stood quietly by the old woman and pecked her food.

When Hanne had finished eating, Mem Pockets gathered the morning eggs, chattering happily to the hens. She thanked the hens for their fine eggs.

"Enjoy your breakfast, my darlings," she said. "I'll leave the door open, and when you are finished, you can scratch about in the gardens."

Mem Pockets took the eggs to the egghouse and carefully placed them in wire egg baskets. The wire baskets allowed the eggs to breathe before she took them to Market.

Every Friday Mem Pockets rose from her bed at five o'clock in the morning. She packed the egg basket carefully with dozens of speckled eggs. She and

Daisy walked two miles to the village of Skara Bree to sell the eggs in the Market Place.

Skara Bree was an ancient village. Most of the houses and buildings were built of stone with red- or green-tiled roofs. Many canals ran through the village. Sturdy stone bridges crossed the canals from one street to another. In the center of the village, beside one of the canals, was the Market.

In the Market everyone called Mem Pockets the Egg Lady. Her eggs were the finest in the islands. In no time at all Mem Pockets sold all but one egg. She always saved the last egg.

Then Mem Pockets and Daisy did their shopping. She bought fresh fruit and cheese for herself, baked biscuits for Daisy, and crushed oyster shells for her hens. She bought the oyster shells from a young boy named Oother, who delivered the shells to the farm at the end of the day. The coarsely ground oyster shells were eaten with great relish by the hens, and helped the hens lay eggs with strong shells.

The last stop that Mem Pockets and Daisy made was at Hobson's Sweets Shop. In exchange for the last egg the old woman bought five pieces of babblers. Babblers were small cubes of hard, brown sugar that she loved to suck when she drank her coffee.

Mem Pockets and Daisy left the village and walked home. Upon arriving at the farm, she gave the hens their special treat of crushed oyster shells and sang them an egg-laying song. While the hens ate, she told them about her day at the Market. Hanne especially loved listening to the stories of the Market.

That evening Mem Pockets and Daisy ate their evening meal and sat quietly reading by the fire. A babbler clattered behind the old woman's teeth as she sipped her coffee.

And so life went peacefully along.

One misty, gray day in October a short, squat stranger, dressed in a large black hat and coat, arrived at the farm. He strode briskly to the front door and rapped loudly with his walking stick.

"Is anyone to home?" he called.

Mem Pockets opened the front door and stared at the stranger.

"Aye. It is myself who is to home."

The stranger took a large brown envelope from his leather satchel and handed it to Mem Pockets. The envelope looked important and had several official-looking stamps and wax seals on it.

"Good day," said the man. He tipped his hat, clicked his heels, and left.

"Whatever can this be?" said Mem Pockets. Daisy sniffed the envelope and whined softly. Mem Pockets slowly opened the envelope. Inside was a letter written on heavy cream paper. The letter read:

Dear Mem Pockets:

It is our sad duty to inform you that the back taxes on your farm have not been paid. If you do not, or cannot, pay the owing taxes within thirty days of receipt of this letter, we regret to inform you that you will lose your farm. We hope that you are able to attend to this matter quickly and save your farm.

Sincerely,
The Gentlemen of Island Taxes

Mem Pockets stared at the letter in disbelief. Her hand flew to her mouth and she gasped softly, "Daisy! We are going to lose the farm. I don't have the money to pay the back taxes." Daisy whimpered and nuzzled the old woman's hand. "Whatever are we going to do?"

Mem Pockets sat and stared into the fire. She could not believe that anyone could actually take her farm from her. The ancient farm had been in her family for hundreds of years. She was a forgetful woman, whose thoughts were often elsewhere, and she had not remembered that the farm taxes had not been paid.

"Oh, Daisy," she said. "I don't know what to do."

Mem Pockets clasped and unclasped her hands. She stood up, straightened her apron, and put on her wide-brimmed yellow hat with its faded red ribbon.

"The hens must be told."

Mem Pockets took the egg basket down from its peg and opened the front door. The mists swirled thickly around the small farm, hiding the henwoodie from view. She slowly made her way through the fog. Daisy quietly followed.

The hens were snug and safe in the henwoodie. Several hens scratched in the fresh straw that Mem Pockets had strewn on the floor the day before. Some sat in their nesting boxes. Others perched on the roost preening their feathers.

When Mem Pockets opened the door, she was greeted with a chorus of excited clucking. The hens loved their mistress and were always glad to see her. It was time for their afternoon meal. And it was time for Mem Pockets to gather the afternoon eggs.

Mem Pockets had brought no meal for the hens. The hens waited expectantly, but no grain was poured into the feed trough. The old woman looked at the hens and wrung her hands. The small black hen stared at her and cocked her head to one side as if trying to read the old woman's thoughts.

"Oh, my dears," said Mem Pockets. "We are going to lose the farm."

The hens stopped clucking. They quietly listened to every word the old woman told them about the letter and the unpaid taxes owed on the farm.

"I'm not certain if you understand what I'm telling you," she said. "I'm not certain I understand it myself."

Mem Pockets gathered the eggs, placed them in her basket, thanked the hens, and left the henwoodie. She did not put the eggs in the wire baskets to breathe. The old woman left the eggs in the basket and trudged back to the house.

"Daisy, I am not very hungry tonight," she said. "But here's a nice bowl of stew for you."

Daisy sniffed the fragrant stew but did not eat. She did not take her eyes from Mem Pockets. The old woman looked small and frail as she sat in her favorite chair gazing into the fire. Mem Pockets sighed and wiped away a tear.

After a while, Mem Pockets blew out the lamp. She and Daisy slowly climbed the stairs to bed.

Outside it began to rain. Mem Pockets lay in bed listening to the rain drumming on the roof. The roof leaked, and a small wooden bucket caught the drips.

Meanwhile, in the henwoodie, the hens held a meeting.

Chapter Two

THE HENS MAKE A DECISION

"LOSE THE FARM!" cried Rose Madder. "We cannot let Mem Pockets lose the farm."

"No, we cannot," said Gemma. "Our mothers and their mothers and their mothers before them lived on this farm for as long as the stone buildings have stood."

"No, we cannot let Mem Pockets lose the farm," said Pyn softly. "But what can we do? We are only hens."

"We must do something!" clucked Maille. "Mem Pockets has always been kind and generous to us."

"We must help her save the farm," said Sophie.

The hens agreed that they must do something to help Mem Pockets save the farm. They clucked and fussed and discussed the matter at great length late into the night. Two hens sat silent, listening to the debate—Old Pegotty, the oldest and wisest hen in the flock; and Hanne, the youngest and smallest hen.

The rain pounded hard on the slate roof. A flash of lightning lit the interior of the henwoodie. Hanne huddled in the corner and ducked her head.

The midnight hour was upon them. Old Pegotty cleared her throat and fluffed her feathers.

"I have something to say," she said. "Quiet, please."

The hens stopped clucking and cackling and stared at the old hen. They waited for her to continue speaking.

Old Pegotty's speckled feathers were faded and gray. She had several bald patches on her breast. Old Pegotty smoothed her thin feathers back into place and looked around at the small flock of hens clustered on the roost.

"In the ancient days, many, many years before any of us were hatched, many years before Mem Pockets was born, the Dragons, who some say were our forefathers, passed on a deep secret to the first Scaldy hens in these islands."

The hens stared at her wide-eyed and held their breath.

"My great-great-great-great-grandmother Hembry Myn told me the secret that only a handful of Scaldy hens know."

The old hen cocked her head as if daring any hen to speak. Not one hen stirred a feather. The storm outside raged on, and the rain thrummed upon the roof.

"Come closer," said Old Pegotty. "This is a secret that no one but us hens must share."

The hens pressed in closer so that their bodies formed a tight circle around the eldest hen.

"Long ago, the Dragons possessed great magic that can still be felt throughout the islands," she said. "And to the hens they gave one Great Mystery—the Secret of Koobi Flora—the Secret of Laying Golden Eggs."

The hens gasped and began to talk at once.

"Silence, please!" said Old Pegotty. "Not all Scaldy hens can lay golden eggs. It is one of the Great Mysteries in the islands. If a hen is hatched during the darkest phase of the moon, the New Moon, that hen's Fate is that she might be chosen to lay three golden eggs."

The old hen looked around at the gathered flock with a sharp eye.

"To be chosen, the hen hatched at the time of the New Moon must prove her worthiness and pass three trials. If Mem Pockets had three golden eggs, she could save the farm, and us, too."

The hens sat in stunned silence. They stared unblinkingly at Old Pegotty.

Lay golden eggs! They had never heard of such a thing. In the old stories of the islands they had heard of a goose that laid golden eggs, but never hens. Hens were ordinary farm fowl with no magic about them whatsoever. Scaldy hens laid the most beautiful eggs in the islands, but not golden eggs.

The hens began talking at once. Lightning flashed outside the window. Thunder rumbled overhead. The rain pelted hard upon the roof of the hen-woodie. Old Pegotty sat quietly and waited.

"Hush," she said. "Hush now and listen carefully to what I have to say."

Again the henwoodie was silent. Only the steady rain could be heard.

"First, we must discover if one among us was hatched during the proper phase of the moon. Her Fate will determine whether she might accomplish the task of laying the golden eggs. If the farm is to be saved, the hen who is chosen must not fail in her quest. Her own life will be placed in great peril to save Mem Pockets and the rest of us."

"But who among us could lay golden eggs?" asked Sophie.

"According to the ancient rhyme taught by the Dragons it must be a hen who is bravest of heart, purest in thought, and wisest in the ways of the Great Goddess," said Old Pegotty. "She must be a hen that was hatched at the time of the New Moon."

Old Pegotty pulled herself up and shook her wattles.

"Now then, who was hatched at the time of the New Moon?" she asked. "Each of us knows our exact hour of hatching because Mem Pockets keeps a log of each egg when it hatches."

The hens clucked softly among themselves.

"Not I," said Rose Madder. "I was hatched when the moon was full."

"Not I," said Gemma. "I was hatched when the moon was waning."

"Not I," said Pyn. "I was hatched when the moon was waxing."

"Not I, not I, not I," said the hens as they thought back to when they first broke free of their egg. They clucked and murmured among themselves, shaking their heads, scratching their thoughts.

"I was hatched at the time of the New Moon," a small voice said from the darkest corner of the henwoodie.

Again the hens stopped clucking and fussing. They stared at the small black hen that had spoken. It was Hanne, the youngest, the quietest, and the smallest hen.

"Ah, Hanne," said Old Pegotty. "Are you certain you were hatched at the time of the New Moon?"

"Yes," said Hanne. "I remember Mem Pockets telling me how exciting it was to have an egg hatch out at the time of the New Moon." Hanne paused. "She said it was the most magical moment for an egg to hatch."

The hens stared in amazement at Hanne. It seemed strange that of all the hens in the henwoodie, she should be the one that hatched under the New Moon. The little hen lowered her head.

"Hanne," said Old Pegotty quietly. "Are you willing to help Mem Pockets save the farm?"

"Yes, of course, I am," replied Hanne. "But . . . but I don't know how."

Old Pegotty fluffed her feathers once more and looked hard at the tiny hen.

"I will tell you how," she said. "And you must do everything exactly as I tell it to you. Do you understand?"

Hanne nodded.

"If you fail in this great task, it will bring doom upon us all, especially dear Mem Pockets."

Then Old Pegotty closed her eyes and began to recite the ancient rhyme that she had been taught many years ago.

The bravest hen must to the ancient barrow go
Through earth and stone, seek the ancient bones
And place upon them the fallen rings
She must beware the barrow-wight
In her heart she must be brave
In the barrow she must eat

Three grains three from the Old Ones' meat.

The purest hen must to the Standing Stones go
Over tarn and field, seek the ancient breath
And feel its strength in stone
She must beware the false winds that blow
In her heart she must be pure
At the Standing Stones she must eat
Three grains three from the Hidden Ones' meat.

The wisest hen must to the Great Green Sea go
Under moon and stars, seek the pounding surf
And hear its mighty voice
She must beware the treacherous tides
In her heart she must be wise
From the salty shore she must eat
Three grains three from the Sea God's meat.

When Old Pegotty had finished speaking, a heavy hush held the hens in awe. "Hanne, are you still willing to help Mem Pockets?" she asked. "The task before you is filled with uncertainty and danger. Hanne, you may not succeed in your quest. Indeed, my dear, you might not return to us at all."

The hens held their breath. Hanne sat upright and raised her head. She looked at the flock watching her intently. Many of the faces showed great fear

after hearing the ancient words of the Dragons that had been passed on to the first Scaldy hens. Hanne turned and faced Old Pegotty.

"I am one small hen. I can only try my best to help Mem Pockets," she said. "I will go to the ancient barrow. I will seek the Standing Stones. I will endure the Great Green Sea. And I will eat the three grains three. Nine times I will eat, and with the blessing of the Great Goddess I will return to this farm and I shall lay the golden eggs."

Secretly, Hanne wondered how she would be able to do all these things.

The rain no longer fell. Outside the henwoodie the night was black and still.

"Hanne, the quest before you will be a difficult and dangerous one," said Old Pegotty gently. "We all know you are the purest. I believe with all my heart that you will be brave. And through your words great wisdom shines bright. Many long years ago there was another prophecy that foretold the fate of a boy who went off-island—It said that he was 'born very old at a very young age.' I think the same may be said of you."

Hanne shivered on the roost. Pyn and Sophie pressed their bodies closer to hers, offering their strength and warmth.

"At the break of day you must begin your quest. You will have one cycle of the moon to complete the task set before you. May the Great Goddess guide you and protect you," said Old Pegotty.

With those words the flock settled down to an uneasy sleep. A sleep filled with dread, foreboding, and the thinnest ray of hope.

"Come, Hanne," said Old Pegotty. "You must learn the rhyme by heart."

The two hens, one old and worn, the other young and sleek, sat huddled by the window. Line by line, Old Pegotty taught Hanne the ancient rhyme.

"Hanne, there is one last thing that you must remember: It is the foolish hen who is caught by the sly fox."

In the wee hours of morning the old hen was satisfied that the young hen knew the rhyme by heart. Old Pegotty softly pecked at the side of Hanne's beak, tucked her head under her wing, and fell into a deep sleep.

Hanne, perched on the roost nearest the window, was unable to sleep. She stared out the window and watched the gray clouds scuttle across the black sky. It was the night of the New Moon, and so no moon sailed across the night sky.

One by one the stars peeped out of the blackness. Against the black sky the Seven Sister Stars twinkled and danced. As Hanne watched, a glimmering star streaked across the sky. Was it a sign? A sign that she might succeed in her quest to save Mem Pockets and the farm?

Chapter Three

THE BARROW

AT DAYBREAK HANNE squeezed through a small crack in the wall and set off. The hens watched silently as she disappeared into the early morning mists. Each hen said a prayer to the Great Goddess to protect the little hen and bring her safely back to the farm. At the edge of the farm Hanne turned and looked back at the snug, warm buildings one last time.

Will I ever see the farm again? she wondered.

The henwoodie was swallowed by thick mists and disappeared.

Mem Pockets and Daisy arrived at the henwoodie to give the hens their breakfast. The old woman looked worn and tired.

"Good morning, my darlings," said Mem Pockets.

The hens were quieter than usual. Mem Pockets saw immediately that one hen was missing.

"Where is Hanne?" she asked. "Where has she gone?"

The hens did not answer. They bowed their heads and did not eat. Mem Pockets dropped the egg basket and wrung her hands. The loss of one of her beloved speckled hens was almost too much for her to bear. None of the hens could explain that Hanne had set off on an impossible quest. That the small black hen was the only hope of saving the farm.

Mem Pockets and Daisy slowly walked back to the house. The hens watched them until they were gone from view.

"Be strong," whispered Old Pegotty.

The hens did not know whether she meant Mem Pockets or Hanne.

Hanne followed a small stream along the western edge of the farm. She knew that the ancient barrow lay to the north of the farm. Mem Pockets and Daisy had often spoken of the barrow with great interest. Hanne wondered what a barrow looked like.

"The bravest hen must to the ancient barrow go," Hanne whispered to herself. She stood for a moment and took her bearings.

The little hen walked northward. She clambered over gnarled roots poking up through the tangled grasses. She hopped over low stone walls. As the mists began to clear, she heard the sounds of wild creatures stirring in the fields. Hanne was careful to keep a sharp eye out for foxes and other dangers.

Hanne walked all morning, keeping the sun to her right. She pecked in the dirt and ate whatever small bits of grain she could find. The little hen drank from a small stream, scooping up the cold water in her beak and throwing back her head to let it slide down her throat. On and on she kept walking north.

"The barrow is much farther than I thought," she said to herself. Hanne wondered if she was heading in the right direction.

By late afternoon, just when she thought she might never reach the barrow, Hanne saw a long, grass-covered mound in the distance. It was the barrow.

It's much larger than I imagined, she thought.

As Hanne drew nearer, the barrow loomed over her. She stood in its shadow and stared up at the immense mound. It was huge! Hanne had never seen a barrow before. She wondered how to get inside. Hanne walked around the mound, exploring. The barrow was enormous, and it took the small hen three-quarters of an hour to reach the spot where she had started her exploration.

Hanne stood and collected her thoughts. She recited the first part of Old Pegotty's rhyme to herself, hoping it would help her discover a way to get inside the barrow.

The bravest hen must to the ancient barrow go
Through earth and stone, seek the ancient bones
And place upon them the fallen rings
She must beware the barrow-wight
In her heart she must be brave
In the barrow she must eat
Three grains three from the Old Ones' meat.

But how do I get inside? she thought.

As Hanne stood staring up at the barrow, she heard a soft scrabbling sound in the grass near her. She cocked her head to one side and listened.

There it was again! Then, quite unexpectedly, a small pink snout and two large fleshy paws popped out of the ground. The snout sneezed. It was a mole.

Hanne leaned forward to better see the tiny creature.

"Hello," she said.

The mole froze at the sound of the hen's voice. Hanne watched as it sniffed the air, trying to catch the scent of whoever it was that was speaking. She hoped her scent did not smell threatening.

"Good day to yerself, miss," said the mole politely. He squinted up at Hanne.

The hen lowered her head closer to the mole.

"I beg your pardon," she said. "But do you live near here? Near this barrow, I mean."

"Och, aye, miss," said the mole. "Right here beneath the barrow, in fact."

The mole scrabbled free of the damp earth and shook bits of clinging dirt and grass from his fine fur.

"I am the Keeper of the Barrow," he said.

Hanne found this news interesting. She thought it odd that the keeper of so large a mound should be so small.

"My name is Hanne," she said. "I am on a quest to save Mem Pockets and the farm. I must get inside the barrow. Do you know where the entrance is?"

The wee mole was silent and appeared to be thinking long and hard about this question from the strange little hen.

"Well, miss," said the mole. "My name is Pieter. As I said, I'm the Keeper of the Barrow." Pieter scratched behind his head for a moment. "Ye cannot go barging into a barrow just to take a quick look-see 'round."

"Oh, I don't want a quick look-see 'round," said Hanne. "I must find the ancient bones and the fallen rings and put the rings back on the fingers. It is the only way to save our farm."

Hanne did not really want to go inside the barrow. Her skin prickled, and for the first time she felt uncertain.

"Och, aye," said the mole. "That is a conundrum now, isn't it." The mole sniffed at the hen. "Hmm . . . let me think now. Ye seem to have a just cause to go inside the barrow. I do not think ye would disturb the bones. In fact, I know exactly where the rings lie that ye speak of."

"You do?" whispered Hanne. "Could you show me the way inside."

The wee mole wiped his nose on the grass and sneezed.

"Are ye no' afraid of the dark?" he asked in a somber voice. "It is black as pitch inside, and there will be no light except what little that leaks in through the low entrance."

This information took Hanne by surprise. She had never been alone in the dark before. The hens had always roosted close by at night in the henwoodie. Her heart fluttered at the thought of going into the barrow alone where it was black as pitch. She wondered what *pitch* was.

Hanne's thoughts turned to Mem Pockets and the other hens that were counting on her to succeed in her quest.

"No, I am not afraid of the dark. Well, I suppose I am a little," she said meekly. "But I must get inside the barrow. Could you come with me?"

"Och, but o' course, miss!" said Pieter enthusiastically. "I love the old barrow. The dark holds no fears for me."

The two tiny figures made their way to the other side of the mound. On the east side of the barrow was a low, stone-built entrance, nearly completely hidden by the overgrown grass. The stones were covered with lichen and moss. Beneath the lintel gaped a small black hole.

It was the entrance to the barrow.

And it was black as pitch, just as Pieter had said.

Pieter scrabbled up to the entrance and sniffed back over his shoulder to make certain Hanne was following, then disappeared into the darkness.

Hanne hesitated for a moment. She took a deep breath, mustered all the courage she could, and darted behind him into the dark hole. It *was* pitch black inside. Blacker than she had ever imagined darkness could be.

The little hen's heart raced with an unknown fear. Her courage began to ebb. Just as she was about to turn and flee from the barrow, Pieter's voice called out.

"Are ye there, miss? I warned ye that it would be dark. But do not panic. Your eyes will adjust in a bit. Things will not look quite as black as ye imagine."

The mole sneezed.

"Always remember that, miss," he said as he wiped his snout on his forearm. "Things are never as black as they may seem."

As Hanne's eyes slowly adjusted to the darkness, she could make out the rough stone walls of the passageway. Pieter was right. It was not as black inside as she had first thought.

"Follow my voice, miss," said the mole. "I will lead ye to the main chamber."

Hanne scurried through the darkness toward the mole's voice.

"It *is* dark in here," said Hanne.

"There has been no light in this barrow for thousands of years," Pieter said. "No one comes to the old barrow anymore. All the treasure has been taken away. Only the ancient man-bones remain, crouched in their deep sleep."

Hanne shuddered at the thought of man-bones. She shook her wattles and puffed out her feathers. She felt very small in the darkness of the barrow.

"Och, but don't ye worry, miss," Pieter said cheerfully. "The rings ye seek are still here. They were too small for anyone to take any notice of. I know right where they lie."

But I am worried, Hanne thought to herself.

Hanne and Pieter had made their way to the central chamber of the barrow. Large upright slabs of stone supported the roof. The barrow had a cold, deathly smell.

"The rings are at the farthest end," said Pieter.

Hanne could see the outlines of stones. In the murky light the great upright slabs looked like great, hulking giants.

Pieter reached the corner and began scrabbling about on the floor.

Hanne squinted her eyes and peered through the dim light. All around she saw the pale patches of white strewn about the floor.

"Och, miss," said Pieter. "Bones."

She cautiously touched a bone with her outstretched foot. The bone crumbled to dust.

The little hen jumped back in alarm and knocked the mole off his feet.

"Oh, Pieter," said Hanne. "I'm sorry, but . . ."

"Och, never ye mind, miss," he said. "But ye might want to scratch about a bit and help me look for the rings."

Hanne began scratching in the hard dirt floor. She threw bits of stone and bone to the side as she scratched and pecked, hoping to find the rings.

Pieter dug several small holes in a row.

Hanne's hopes began to fade.

Where were the rings? she wondered. How would she ever find them in the darkness of the barrow?

"Here they be, miss!" he shouted. "Three rings of man. Just like I told ye there would be."

Hanne ran to where Pieter had dug his holes.

"Where are they?" she asked.

Hanne craned her neck so that she could better see. In the blurred darkness she could see the bright glimmer of gold.

"Och, right there in front of yer very beak," said Pieter.

And so they were.

"Master Pieter, thank you," she said. "I would never have found these rings in the blackness on my own."

Hanne lifted each ring out of the hole and piled them at her feet.

"Now, miss," said Pieter. "What did ye say ye wanted to do with the rings?"

Hanne squeezed her eyes shut and tried to remember the ancient rhyme that Old Pegotty had taught her. She recited the first part of the rhyme aloud.

The bravest hen must to the ancient barrow go
Through earth and stone, seek the ancient bones
And place upon them the fallen rings
She must beware the barrow-wight
In her heart she must be brave
In the barrow she must eat
Three grains three from the Old Ones' meat.

Pieter listened to the words. He scrunched up his nose and sneezed.

Hanne jumped. Her squawk echoed in the barrow. At the sound of Hanne's squawk Pieter tumbled over backward. He began to laugh.

"Well, miss," he said as he brushed off his fur. "Ye gave me a bit of a start there just now."

"I'm sorry," said Hanne. "I didn't mean to frighten you."

"Och, no bother," said the mole. "Those words ye said about the barrow-wight made me remember something I had not thought of for a long while now. Let me think on it a moment."

Hanne stood quietly beside the little mole while he snuffled and thumped the floor with his foot. The air inside the barrow seemed to grow colder.

Is it getting darker in here? Hanne asked herself.

"I've got it!" cried Pieter. "I had nearly forgotten about the hidden chamber down at the other end of the barrow. It is quite small, and no one has been inside it except for meself."

"There's another chamber besides this one?" Hanne asked.

"Och, aye," said Pieter. "I have not bothered much about it because it seemed safe enough to be left alone. Inside the secret chamber are more man-bones, a complete skeleton. If I understand yer rhyme right enough, it is there that ye must take the rings and place them on the bones of that dead man."

Hanne trembled. It sounded simple enough. She would take the rings, one by one in her beak, and place them on the dead man's fingers. The little hen was beginning to feel uneasy in the oppressive darkness and wanted to get out as quickly as possible.

"There's one part of the rhyme I don't understand," said Hanne thoughtfully. "What does it mean, 'beware the barrow-wight'?"

Pieter sat in silence beside her.

"Well, miss," he said slowly. "The barrow-wight is the ghost of the bones of that man-skeleton. Sometimes it gets agitated like and moans and groans something pitiful."

Hanne gasped and sat down hard on the floor.

"I have never seen it, mind," said Pieter. "But I have heard him wailing on cold, lonely nights. His moaning is enough to wake the dead and make the blood run right out of yer toes."

Hanne shivered. She knew about ghosts. Mem Pockets had told the hens that the farmhouse had a ghost that rattled the pots and pans and blew out the candles. Hanne thought ghosts sounded like troublesome, restless creatures that had nothing better to do than scare the living.

"I am not afraid of ghosts," said Hanne. "One barrow-wight does not frighten me."

"Och, miss," said Pieter gravely. "Ye don't know barrow-wights. They can be a fearsome terror and make ye drop dead in yer tracks."

Hanne's heart thumped. If she dropped dead in her tracks, Mem Pockets would certainly lose the farm and the hens would be doomed. She would *not* drop dead in her tracks, no matter how much the barrow-wight moaned.

Inside the barrow the darkness grew blacker. Hanne could hear the mole's soft breathing. Nothing stirred.

"Master Pieter," said Hanne. "The three grains three. Where will I find them?"

"If I remember a-right, in the chamber there is a small bowl," said Pieter. "And in the bowl there are three grains, left there for the barrow-wight."

"Well, there's nothing else to do but go into that chamber," said the small hen.

She hoped she sounded braver than she felt.

"Remember, miss," he said. "Nothing is ever as black as it seems."

Hanne took a deep breath and picked up the first gold ring. She and Pieter cautiously crept to the other end of the chamber. In one corner the darkness seemed blacker than anywhere else.

"That is the entrance to the secret chamber," whispered Pieter. "It is in there ye must go, miss."

"Aren't you coming with me?" asked Hanne. The glittering ring fell to the floor.

"Och, no, miss," said Pieter. "It is something ye must do by yerself. This is yer task, not mine. I've helped ye as much as I can, now ye must carry on alone."

Hanne knew that Pieter spoke the truth. It was her task to save the farm.

Hanne picked up the ring once more and ducked inside the secret chamber. It smelled dank and moldy. She strained to see in the blackness. Hanne could see nothing. Nothing at all. She felt with her feet. Her foot touched something hard and smooth. It was bone—cold, dead bone.

Hanne's heart pounded. She tapped the bone with her foot. It was long and twisted. At one end she felt smaller bones. She examined the bones with her toes. They formed the shape of a man's hand.

Hanne held her breath. She poked the finger bones with her beak and niggled the ring onto the skeleton's smallest finger. Then she scuttled out of the stifling chamber.

Without a word to Pieter she ran back to the remaining two rings. She picked up the second ring and slipped into the secret chamber again. Hanne worked the ring onto the fourth finger of the skeleton's clenched hand.

Hanne sped out, ran to the opposite end of the central chamber, and picked up the last ring. It felt heavier than the other two.

Pieter listened and held his breath as he heard her enter the chamber for the third time. Hanne quickly placed the third ring on the dead man's middle finger. As soon as the ring was on the dead finger, she heard a faint rustling sound.

The bones were stirring.

Hanne froze. She spun around and was just about to dart out of the chamber, away from the restless bones, when she heard Pieter's voice. It sounded very far away.

"Miss," he called. "Do not forget to eat the three grains."

The grains! thought Hanne. I almost forgot to eat the three grains.

She scrambled and scratched in the blackness until she found a small bowl lying at the skeleton's feet. Hanne pecked at the bottom of the bowl. There were three grains.

Hanne quickly ate the first grain. It was dry and tasted like the earth. She heard a soft shuffling nearby. She ate the second grain. It was hard and tasted like stone. Just as she was about to eat the third grain, a low, rumbling moaning surrounded her. The little hen's blood ran cold. Her body went rigid with fright. The dank air in the tiny chamber was suddenly deathly cold.

Hanne could not move, could not think what to do.

From deep within her memory she heard Old Pegotty's voice: *Hanne, you must not fail or we shall be doomed.*

Hanne quickly ate the last grain. It was damp and tasted salty. She had barely swallowed the third grain when the moaning grew louder. Icy cold, bony fingers grasped her by the legs.

"Death is your reward for being such a foolish hen," said a thin voice in her ear.

The barrow-wight's rotted fingers gripped her legs tighter and tighter. The three gold rings shimmered brightly in the blackness.

"It is done!" she cried. "I have placed the fallen rings on your fingers. I have eaten the three grains three. Be still, and leave me in peace."

The eerie, bloodcurdling moaning stopped. The dead fingers released her legs. Hanne's breath came in gasps. She darted out of the silent chamber.

"Run!" she cried to Pieter.

Pieter sniffed at the little hen.

"Run?" he asked. "But why?"

"The barrow-wight is after me," she cried. "And he'll get you, too! Run!"

Hanne and Pieter ran for their lives. A terrible screech nearly made them drop dead in their tracks. They scampered through the central chamber, down the narrow passage to the entrance, and out of the barrow into the blinding daylight. The two companions collapsed into the grass, panting.

"Well, miss," said Pieter. "Just imagine! Talking to a barrow-wight like that. I would have never done it meself."

"I don't know why I said those words," said Hanne. "They just came into my head. We must have been inside the barrow for ages."

"Och, no, miss," Pieter said. "We were in there for just a wee while. Look. The sun has hardly moved at all."

"Master Pieter, you must be very brave," Hanne said quietly. "To live in darkness all the time and to tend the dead inside the barrow. I don't think I would choose such a task."

"Och, miss," said Pieter. "I did not choose to be the Keeper of the Barrow. It is my Fate. I do it because I must. Jus' like yerself having to go inside the barrow to find the rings and eat the grains. It is all the same. We cannot choose our Fate in this world. We can only do our best and get on with it."

Hanne nodded her head. She shook out her feathers, and dust flew all around her. She understood.

They sat in silence beside the barrow. She had not chosen to go on the quest to save the farm. She had not chosen to go into the barrow to get the rings, to face the barrow-wight. It had all been thrust upon her at the oddest moment.

But she could not let Mem Pockets lose the farm. She could not let the other hens be doomed. And it was time to get on with it.

"Master Pieter," said Hanne. "Do you know the way to the Standing Stones?" The little mole raised his head and sniffed the air.

"West, miss," Pieter said. "The Standing Stones lie to the west of the barrow. Just follow the path of the sun and ye'll come to them." He paused. "And don't forget what I told you, things are never quite as black as they may seem."

"I shall always remember you, Master Pieter."

"And I, you, miss," said the mole.

Pieter winked his tiny eye at the little hen.

Hanne stood and stretched her legs. She opened her beak to speak again, but the little mole shook his head.

"I know, miss," he said quietly. "Ye do not have to say it."

The wee mole sprang to his feet and shook himself vigorously.

"Off ye go!" he said. "May you succeed in yer quest and save the farm. It must be a grand place indeed. I should like to visit it one day."

Pieter rubbed his snout with his forepaw.

"Ye are the bravest hen, miss. Without a doubt, that ye are."

As suddenly as he had appeared, the tiny mole disappeared into the earth.

Hanne turned and headed west toward the Standing Stones. She was a different hen than she had been at the beginning of her extraordinary adventure.

Chapter Four

THE STANDING STONES

HANNE'S MIND RACED as she pushed her way through the dry grass. Her experience in the barrow had been frightening, but she had never abandoned hope. She had fulfilled the first task set before her.

"And I did not drop dead in my tracks," she clucked.

As she walked, Hanne's thoughts returned to the farm and Mem Pockets. Her entire life on the farm had been spent quietly pecking in the farmyard and scratching in the gardens with the other hens.

Hanne loved the farm's solid stone buildings with their gray slate roofs. There were rambling stone walls with secret places filled with mystery and surprises. In the barn there was fragrant hay in which she liked to sit and look out at the farm. The gardens were Hanne's favorite place to scratch in the earth and find delicious things to eat. The farm had always been her home.

Hanne loved Mem Pockets most of all. She was a short, plump woman whose step the hens eagerly listened for every morning. Mem Pockets fed the hens and fussed over them. The old woman stroked their heads and sang to them as she gathered the eggs. She told them exciting news about the village and the mysterious place where she took their eggs every Friday called the Market.

The Market sounded like a fabulous place to Hanne. She longed to visit it and see all the wondrous sights for herself.

Throughout the year Mem Pockets made certain that all the animals on the farm were comfortable and well fed. She celebrated Daisy's birthday with a party for all the animals and her neighbors.

Whenever one of the animals died, Mem Pockets was deeply saddened. She buried her lost friends under a large oak tree behind the barn. Mem Pockets often sat quietly beneath the tree's branches remembering those that had died. They would never be forgotten.

On Midsummer's Eve Mem Pockets baked special oatcakes for the animals and hens. In the cold winter months she kept the animals and hens snug and warm. At the Winter Solstice the old woman sat up all night with the hens and told them about the Mystery of the Death of the Old Year.

Hanne felt homesick for Mem Pockets and the farm.

As the day wore on, Hanne walked a considerable distance. The outside world was an enormous place to the small hen. She was grateful for Pieter's advice in guiding her in the right direction to the Standing Stones.

Hanne stopped and rolled in the dirt, dusting her feathers. She carefully preened them back into place before setting off again. The little hen felt a pang of hunger.

I do miss Mem Pockets bringing food, she thought as she scrambled over the rocks and heather roots.

Hanne watched as the sun began to slip behind the rocky crags. Soon it would be gone. She had never spent the night outdoors. She had never slept alone. Hanne wondered where she would sleep and if she would be safe from foxes.

As dusk fell, the little hen knew she must find a safe place to roost for the night. She looked around and saw nothing but stumpy, gnarled willow trees growing beside an old canal. She saw stone walls surrounding the fields, but she did not see a suitable place for a hen to roost for the night. Hanne knew that there were too many dangers and unknown predators for her to sleep on the ground.

As the last rays of the setting sun dipped behind the rocks, Hanne saw an unused windmill in the distance.

I suppose it will have to do, she thought to herself.

Hanne ran as quickly as she could toward the windmill. She reached the windmill safely and looked about. Its conical roof had gaping holes. Its sails were tattered and hung in limp rags on the frames. The broken frames looked like bleached fish bones against the darkening sky. The doorway had no door, and the little hen peered cautiously inside. Foxes liked unused buildings to use for their dens.

The windmill was filled with rusting gears and cranks. There was a musty, floury smell, and a thick layer of dust covered everything. Hanne looked up and saw wooden rafters.

"Perfect!" she said. "I can roost on the rafters and sleep peacefully tonight."

Hanne scrambled up to the rafters. She tiptoed to the center of a wide oak beam, fluffed her feathers, and settled herself for the night. She tucked her head beneath her wing. No one would harm her here.

In the middle of the night Hanne was suddenly wide awake. She had heard a soft scuffling noise below. The windmill was not as dark inside as the barrow had been. By the pale light that slanted through the holes in the roof Hanne saw movement on the floor.

A large dark mass shifted and shuffled in the dust. In the darkness Hanne saw hundreds of red pinpricks shining up at her.

Rats! thought Hanne. Hundreds of rats.

The little hen sat still.

She knew that if the rats heard or smelled her, she was doomed. The rats did not hear or smell the hen perched high above their heads. They had their eyes set on another hapless victim.

Hanne watched in horror as the rats surrounded a small furry animal. It was a water vole. The rats swarmed over it, snarling and gnashing their teeth. The water vole screamed. Hanne squeezed her eyes shut. The scene below was too gruesome to watch.

The little hen spent a sleepless night. She dared not close her eyes, or tuck her head beneath her wing.

Thus Hanne passed her first night alone and away from the farm.

The next morning Hanne found the windmill blanketed in heavy mist. An early frost had settled over the island during the night. She felt cold and stiff after her sleepless night on the rafter. The windmill was not snug and warm like the henwoodie with the other hens clustered around her for warmth and company.

Hanne shook her feathers and stretched her wings and legs. She yawned and flew to the floor. Outside, the ground shimmered in the pale gray light.

Hanne began walking west. She hoped she would reach the Standing Stones before nightfall. As she walked, she scratched in the dirt and found bits of things to eat. She missed the delicious meals that Mem Pockets brought the hens each morning.

Hanne walked that entire day. The mists thinned. She met several friendly, shaggy cows, a noisy flock of sheep, and a timid hedgehog. They were curious that such a small hen was out and about on her own. Whenever Hanne heard a wagon or someone coming along the road, she ducked out of sight behind a stone wall or rock. The little hen instinctively knew that she must not be seen.

Hanne crossed small tarns and soaked her feet in the cold water. She drank deeply from the clear water and felt refreshed. Throughout the day she crossed many fields and scrambled through ancient hedgerows of hawthorn and willow.

The little hen did not reach the Standing Stones on the first day after her sleepless night in the windmill. She marched on for another four days.

On the fifth day after leaving the barrow Hanne began to wonder if she had somehow taken a wrong turn. Each morning she watched the sun rise and headed off in the opposite direction. She always followed the sun in its westward migration across the sky. The little hen had not realized it would take such a long time to reach the Standing Stones.

Hanne stood in the middle of the road, pondering what to do. Suddenly, a dark shadow fell across the road. Her heart skittered, and she quickly darted into the hedgerow. Hanne felt a *whoosh* of wind behind her. Safely hidden in the hedgerow, she peeked out and saw a large black bird swooping past where she had just been standing.

Thank goodness I had the sense to run when I did, she thought wildly.

Old Pegotty had once told her of a hen that had been snatched up by a great black bird and carried off. Hanne shuddered at the thought.

"I shall have to be more alert if I am ever to reach the Standing Stones," she said to herself.

Hanne waited for some time until she was certain it was safe to venture from the hedgerow.

By early afternoon the mists had cleared. The countryside became wilder and was not so well tended. The landscape was filled with great masses of craggy outcrops of stone.

Hanne scampered to a small hillock. She clambered to the top and looked around. To her right she saw nothing but a tangled, overgrown field of heather. To her left she saw three large, gray slabs of stone rising up out of the earth, pointing to the sky like thick fingers.

The Standing Stones!

Hanne had not known what to expect when she found the Standing Stones. She had not asked Pieter how many stones there would be. But in her heart she knew that these were the Standing Stones that she had been seeking.

Hanne ran to the stones as fast as she could. She hoped the black bird would not swoop down on her again. As she ran across the rough ground, a

sharp wind rustled her sleek feathers. Hanne shivered and felt chilled to the bone. She reached the Standing Stones and stared up at them.

The stones stood close together as if huddled in conversation. They were weathered and covered with wisps of pale green lichen. Two of the stones were tall and thin. The third was short and squat.

They were giants!

The barrow had been enormous, but these stones towered over her so that she could barely see the tops. As Hanne moved nearer to the stones, she felt a tingling pass through her feathers. She felt dizzy standing so near the stones.

It was well known throughout the islands that each Standing Stone possessed great power. No one knew from whence this power came. It was simply part of life in the islands.

Hanne took a few more steps closer to the stone nearest her. Her vision blurred and her head reeled. Suddenly the little hen was flung backward and lay stunned on the ground.

This must be the ancient power of the stones, she thought.

The tricksy, chill wind ruffled her feathers more violently. Hanne shivered. The wind made her long for home.

I could turn back now and reach the farm in a few days, Hanne thought. I'm hungry and cold and tired.

The whispery wind wailed in Hanne's ear. She turned and took one step back toward the farm and Mem Pockets.

The wanton wind ruffled her feathers. Hanne's heart longed for home.

"Beware the false winds that blow," said a soft voice.

"Where did that voice come from?" the little hen asked out loud.

Beware the false winds that blow. These words made Hanne think. Then she remembered the second part of the rhyme Old Pegotty had taught her. She spoke the lines to the tricksy wind:

The purest hen must to the Standing Stones go
Over tarn and field, seek the ancient breath
And feel its strength in stone
She must beware the false winds that blow
In her heart she must be pure
At the Standing Stones she must eat
Three grains three from the Hidden Ones' meat.

As Hanne recited the lines, her thoughts cleared and the buzzing in her head stopped. Hanne squeezed her eyes shut to clear her vision. When she opened her eyes, she saw that a thin mist hovered just above the ground. The three Standing Stones had vanished. Three very old, and very odd, creatures stood where the stones had been.

The little hen did not feel afraid. These creatures were extraordinary to look upon, even for a hen. One of the creatures raised its large gnarled hand and beckoned Hanne to come closer. The hand reminded her of Pieter's forepaws.

Their skin looked very much like the rough surface of the stones. Their pale eyes were set deep beneath heavy brows and were filled with great sadness and wisdom. Deep creases crinkled around their eyes, and a large, strong nose sat crookedly in the center of their worn faces.

Each had two long, thin braids that reached nearly to the ground, hanging down either side of her face. All three wore homespun gray-green clothing. Each wore a curving cap.

Hanne hesitated for a moment, then strode bravely toward the three mysterious figures. She stood before them and gazed at their craggy faces.

Hanne did not know whether to speak or not. Would these creatures be able to understand henspeak?

"Well-come, brave Hanne," said the shortest one. She wore a russet red cap on her wide head. Her voice was soft and deep. It was not like Mem Pockets's voice at all. The voice sounded like wintry wind on stone. Nearly breathless.

"I am Grainne. My name means 'That Which Is.' These are my sisters, Nuala—That Which Is Becoming, and Oona—That Which Should Be."

Hanne stared at the remarkable creatures and opened her beak to speak.

"You do not need to speak," said Nuala.

"We know why you have come," said Oona. "Do not be afraid, brave Hanne."

The three figures shuffled forward, never taking their gaze from the small hen. "We are the Oldest Old Ones, or Hidden Ones, as some folk call us. We are three of the five Keepers of the Stones—the Atecotti."

Hanne gasped.

"Do not be afraid, Hanne," said Grainne. "It is a rare thing indeed for us to show ourselves to man or beast or fowl. From the stars and the earth we learned of you and your quest. The Watcher, the mole Pieter, Keeper of the Barrow, sent word that a small black speckled hen would seek our help. We have waited for you to come."

The Atecotti bowed low to the hen.

"Again we say, well-come, brave Hanne."

Hanne's feathers stood on end. The voices of the Atecotti thrilled her. Their voices held her in a spell. She could not stir or run away. Hanne felt quite small and unimportant beside these magical beings.

Grainne spoke to her again.

"Great power is kept in the Standing Stones," she said. "This power comes from the earth and is a gift from the Great Goddess herself. The Dragons channeled the power of the earth and guided us to erect these stones. They have stood for thousands of years."

Hanne bowed her head.

"We hold the grains that you seek, little hen," said Nuala.

As each of the Atecotti pulled a small leather pouch from within the folds of her cloak, the false wind began to blow once more.

Hanne turned her head toward where she thought Mem Pockets and the farm lay behind her.

I could run now and they would never catch me, she thought. Maybe they are foxes in disguise.

"Be calm in your thoughts, Hanne," said Oona. "We are not foxes."

From each pouch the Atecotti took out a single grain.

"Come, Hanne," said Grainne. "We offer you these three grains freely and with all the blessing that we may offer. You are on a dangerous quest. You risk your own life to save others. And that is a great deed."

"Eat these grains and be well fed," said Nuala. "Each of these grains holds great magic that we have bestowed upon them."

"Their power and magic comes from the stones," said Oona.

"These grains will aid you in fulfilling your great quest," said Grainne. "The bravery you have shown will make it possible for the magic to work."

"Come, Hanne," the Atecotti said together.

Hanne hesitated.

Is there really magic in these three grains being offered to me? she thought. In her heart, Hanne knew that the words the Atecotti spoke were true.

Hanne slowly stepped forward.

She ate each grain from the hand of each of the Atecotti. Unlike the three grains she had eaten in the barrow, these grains tasted delicious. They tasted like . . . the farm!

Hanne's toes tingled.

"From here you must continue west to the sea—the Great Green Sea," said Grainne.

"It is not a long journey," said Nuala. "But there are still many dangers and false winds that could confound one small hen such as yourself."

"Keep your wits and heart about you," said Oona. "And you will reach the sea in safety."

"Always be alert to the sly fox," said Grainne. "It is the foolish hen who is caught by the sly fox."

The three Atecotti stepped back. The white mists swirled around them, becoming thicker so that Hanne could barely see them.

Grainne's husky voice spoke again.

"When you reach the sea, you will hear her great thundering voice. Do not be afraid. Wait until the full moon rises and the Seven Sister Stars sit beside her. Then, take from the Sea God's hand the last three grains. Beware the treacherous tides that crave all creatures' souls."

Grainne finished speaking. She held her hand over Hanne's head and murmured an ancient prayer. With her other hand she pointed to the west, toward the sea. Hanne turned and slowly walked away.

Hanne glanced back for one last look at the strange creatures who had shown her such tenderness. But the Atecotti had vanished. Only the thickening mists crept among the three stones that stood where they had been. The mists quickly hid the stones from her sight.

It was twilight—the most magical time between day and night. It was only at twilight that the island's most magical creatures revealed themselves.

But Hanne did not know this. She only knew that once again she must find a safe place to roost. Night was fast upon her.

Through the mists Hanne saw a twisted and bent elder tree. She marched to the tree and flew into its lower branches. She was exhausted and felt safe within its arms.

Hanne's toes gripped the branch hard. No fox or rats would snatch her on this night.

Chapter Five

THE GREAT GREEN SEA

AT DAYBREAK HANNE awoke with the first chirping of the birds. She flew to the ground and once more continued on her journey to the sea. The speckled hen foraged for food wherever she could find it.

For several days Hanne made her way farther and farther west. She was careful to be alert to any dangers. Each day brought new adventures, and each night found her closer to her journey's end.

Every night she watched for the moon. The moon grew larger and larger with each passing night. Hanne wondered if she would reach the Green Sea in time for the full moon and in time to meet the Sea God.

One misty morning Hanne awoke as usual. Something was different. She flew down from her previous night's roost and sniffed the air. The air was different. It smelled tangy and felt thicker on her feathers. Hanne waited for the sun to rise once more. By now it had become her morning ritual to watch for the sun, and she was thankful when it appeared. On the days when it rained, or the mists blanketed the island, she missed the sun's warmth.

Hanne found a few seeds beside the path. She scratched in the earth and ate whatever she could find. The little hen was thinner, lighter than when she had first begun her journey. Hanne took her bearings from the faint glimmers of light through the mists and continued walking west.

She walked briskly and felt a sticky dampness clinging to her feathers. When she preened her feathers, they tasted salty.

How odd, she thought.

The ground began to slope downward. The grasses became coarser. The stones were covered more thickly in lichens. Beneath her feet the soil felt gritty and crunched between her toes. As she walked, she picked up each foot and shook it. Tiny bits of sand stuck to her scaly legs and feet.

In the distance Hanne heard a peculiar sound. It was a dull roaring and crashing. The air felt heavier than ever. When she breathed, she could taste the salty air. The roaring became louder, and her heart pounded with the sound.

The Scaldy hen suddenly found herself standing on the edge of a rocky cliff, looking down upon a wide expanse of bare white earth. It wasn't dirt, it was sand. And where the sand ended, she gazed for the first time at the sea.

"The sea," cried Hanne. "I have reached the Great Green Sea!"

The sea rose and fell upon the sand with a thunderous roar. It seemed to stretch forever. Hanne could see no end to it. For the first time the little hen felt uncertain. How would she ever find the three grains among all the grains of sand by the sea? A loud, raucous cry overhead made Hanne look up.

Large white birds with black-tipped wings and bright yellow beaks circled overhead. Hanne's heart leapt at the thought that these might be hawks. Their shadows on the sand did not look like the shadow of a hawk. Who were these strange birds? She had never seen so many birds flocking together like this.

Hanne stood for a long while watching the seabirds soar and glide over the sand and sea. She had never thought much about flying. The little hen had flown only to reach a safe roosting place at night. But now, as she watched the graceful flight of the seabirds, Hanne longed to soar high above the sea with them.

"I will never find the last three grains if I stand here daydreaming all day," she said to herself. "Oh, I do wish I could fly. Then when I return to the farm I would not have to walk so far. I could fly home in an instant."

Thinking of the farm, the hens, and Mem Pockets brought tears to Hanne's eyes. Her heart felt heavy. Hanne missed the farm.

Hanne carefully picked her way down the steep rocky cliff to the sandy beach. She ran along the beach, heedless of any dangers that might be lurking in the shadows of the large rocks strewn about the sand. The sea seemed to draw her closer and closer. It pulled and tugged at her heart to come to it. Hanne's feet felt the sand suddenly turn cold and wet. She was at the very edge of water.

Hanne jumped back just as a wave crashed in the surf and surged toward her. The sea rushed in, then drained away again.

Up and down the beach Hanne saw brightly colored shells and stones. Long strands of dark, slippery seaweed swirled in the shallows of the sea.

Hard-shelled creatures scurried about the sand among the seaweed and flotsam and jetsam. Hanne was amazed by what she saw and smelled.

But the little black hen felt completely at a loss as to where to begin to search for the last three grains. The wind blew more strongly, and the waves were topped with white foam. Hanne huddled among the rocks at the water's edge and tried to think what to do.

Hanne remembered her last night roosting close to Old Pegotty, learning the rhyme that had guided her throughout her journey. She recited the entire rhyme once more to herself, hoping to find a clue as to how she would find the God of the Sea and the last three grains that she must eat.

The Atecotti had told her that she would have to wait for the full moon and take the three grains from the Sea God's hand.

But what does the Sea God look like? she thought to herself. Where will I find him?

Hanne felt too exhausted to think about this now. She would think about it tomorrow.

Hanne skittered along the water's edge, watching the sea's restless surges. The rocks did not provide much shelter. The sun began to drop lower on the horizon. It was the first time Hanne had watched the sun set over the sea. The sky burned red and merged with the sea on the horizon. As the sun disappeared, the air grew colder. Hanne shivered on the sand and fluffed her feathers, trapping what warmth she could around her body.

Darkness fell. The sea crept closer and closer toward her. Hanne did not know about tides and was unaware that as the full moon rose, the tide would rise with it to its highest level. The little hen had no idea of the grave danger she was in if she stayed where she was.

As she huddled in the darkness, Hanne's thoughts were of Mem Pockets and the hens back on the farm. Were they safe and snug in the henwoodie? She wondered if the hens thought of her. Had any of them ever seen or heard the roar of the sea?

Without warning, Hanne's feet were wet! They were more than wet, they were underwater. Hanne leapt back and flew to the top of one of the rocks between which she had huddled, trying to keep warm.

The sea raced toward her faster and faster, churning around the rocks on which she stood. The little hen scrambled higher up the slippery rock just out of reach of the sea as it crashed around her.

"Keep your wits about you, Hanne," a soft, whispery voice said.

It was Grainne's voice. Hanne gripped the rock with her toes and clung to it with all her strength. Hanne breathed deeply and tried to calm her thoughts. She looked around her and saw the swirling water rising higher and higher. The sea would soon cover the rocks on which she was precariously perched.

Farther up the beach Hanne spied a high clump of grass and sand. She knew that if she was to survive, she must reach higher ground away from the incoming tide. Hanne spread her wings and plunged from the rocks, hoping to make a dash for the safety of higher ground.

A huge wave crashed upon the rocks just as the little hen took flight. The wave caught her and tumbled her into the foaming surf.

The seawater was icy cold. The sea was stronger than she was. As the wave retreated, Hanne kicked her legs and beat her wings against the pull of the sea.

But it dragged her farther and farther away from the safety of the land.

Another gigantic wave broke over her. Hanne opened her beak to cry out, but seawater poured into her mouth. The little hen choked and sputtered. She frantically flapped her wings to free herself from the clinging sea.

Hanne felt the sand and rocks drop away from beneath her. For just a moment she bobbed on the surface of the water. She felt weightless. Her strength began to ebb. She fought the sea with all her might, but one small hen was no match for its awesome power. Hanne felt herself slipping beneath the surface, sinking deeper and deeper into its icy depths.

Unexpectedly, she felt something hard and ridged under her feet. Barely conscious, Hanne felt herself being lifted from below. She instinctively clenched her toes onto the ridged stone.

Hanne's head came out of the water. She gasped as the cold night air filled her lungs. Hanne clung to the stone. It was floating on the sea!

The gigantic stone gently rose and fell with the waves. It swam toward the beach. Hanne held out her wings for balance as the stone swam closer to the shore. She felt a jolt as the stone dragged itself out of the water.

The stone stopped moving. Hanne leapt from it and scrambled away from the water's edge. When she reached dry sand, her legs gave way and she sat down hard. She was exhausted and terrified. Hanne gasped for breath. Her feathers were soaked, and she began to shake.

"You must be watchful of the tides," said a deep, rumbling voice behind her.

Hanne spun around and stared at the most bizarre creature she had ever seen. It was the swimming stone that was speaking to her.

"When the moon rises, the tides race in upon the sands," continued the stone. "The sea grabs whatever it can from the land and drags it down to its cold depths. When the moon is full, the tides rise to their highest and are then the most dangerous."

The swimming stone had a small bald head with tiny heavy-lidded eyes. It lay on the sand with its legs drawn in close to its body. Its legs were scaly like a hen's. The creature's back was domed and shiny wet from the sea. Sand stuck to its surface and gave the creature a mottled appearance. The swimming stone was staring at Hanne.

Hanne wondered if she looked as strange to the stone as he did to her.

"You speak," said Hanne. "How can a swimming stone speak?"

The giant sea turtle stared steadily at the little hen.

"I am not a swimming stone," he said quietly. "I am a living creature, just like yourself. I am what some call a sea turtle, and others call the God of the Sea."

"God of the Sea!" cried Hanne. "Then you are the one I hoped to find."

Hanne stood up on shaky legs. She squeezed her eyes shut and recited the last refrain from the ancient rhyme:

> *The wisest hen must to the Great Green Sea go*
> *Under moon and stars, seek the pounding surf*
> *And hear its mighty voice*
> *She must beware the treacherous tides*
> *In her heart she must be wise*
> *From the salty shore she must eat*
> *Three grains three from the Sea God's meat.*

Treacherous tides! Hanne now realized she should have more carefully considered the words of the rhyme.

What a foolish hen I've been, she thought.

The sea turtle slowly inched his way closer to the hen. He hauled his great bulk along the sand, leaving a deep rut behind him. Hanne moved toward him, and the two stood very close, staring at each other.

The God of the Sea smelled of the sea. He smelled like the oyster shells Mem Pockets fed the hens!

"Thank you for saving my life," said Hanne. "I don't know very much about the sea. It rushed in and pulled me away from the rocks before I could fly away."

"That is the way of the sea," said the turtle. "It often takes without asking. There are many creatures who do not belong in its cold depths."

"You came along just in time," said Hanne.

"I came along, as you say, because the Oldest Old Ones sent word that you were searching for me. And so I came."

Hanne stared in amazement at the ancient turtle.

"But how did the Atecotti send word to you?" Hanne asked. "They are a long way from here."

"Ah," said the old sea turtle. "That is a Mystery that only the Keepers of the Stones and other Watchers may understand. I cannot tell you the secret. It is our gift from the Great Goddess."

Hanne shook her feathers. The sea turtle's nearness made her feel warmer. His shell seemed to radiate heat. Hanne's feathers were quickly drying.

"There is a great deal I don't understand," said Hanne. "I was chosen to make this journey so that Mem Pockets won't lose the farm. If I don't find the last three grains, I will fail in my quest."

"Wisdom begins with the knowledge that there is much to learn," said the sea turtle gravely.

Hanne sat silently beside the sea turtle.

"Wisdom also lies in the Knowing of Names," the old turtle said. "To know someone's true name is to be able to call them. It is a mysterious power."

The old sea turtle closed his eyes and seemed to be resting. Hanne waited for him to continue. At last he spoke.

"I know you are the hen that they call Hanne. It is a noble name indeed. I have told you what they call me, but I shall reveal my true name to you because you have proven yourself worthy. I am called Old Murdaugh—Protector of the Sea. I have journeyed far across the waters from the Misty Isles to meet you."

Hanne stared at the old turtle. She did not know what to say. She wondered how the old sea turtle had known her name. But the little hen dared not ask.

"Since you know my name, then you must know that I must eat the last three grains so that I can help Mem Pockets save the farm," said Hanne softly.

"Aye," said Old Murdaugh. "I know that the success of your quest depends on your bravery, purity, and wisdom."

Old Murdaugh watched the hen closely.

"In the barrow you proved that you are indeed a brave hen who sets aside her fears to help others. In order for the three most powerful Atecotti to appear to you and offer you their aid, you must be pure of heart."

The old sea turtle tilted his head and looked up into the night sky. Overhead, the full moon slowly rose above them. The Seven Sister Stars shone brightly beside her. The sea turtle began scraping in the sand with his huge flippers. As he scraped away the sand, he sang softly—-a strange, mysterious Song of the Sea.

Hanne watched eagerly as he dug deeper and deeper in the damp sand. Soon the old sea turtle had scraped a large hole. Old Murdaugh stared down into the depths of the hole he had dug.

"Now, little hen," he said in a grave voice. "Your greatest trial has come."

The old sea turtle edged closer to the small hen. Hanne trembled from his nearness.

"You must look into the depths of the Sands of Time," said Old Murdaugh. "I cannot tell you which three grains you must eat. Only in your heart can you recognize them among the many thousands of grains at the bottom of this hole."

The old sea turtle stared hard at the little hen.

"How will I ever recognize three tiny grains among the many thousands?" she cried.

"Let the full moon's light guide you," he said. "Listen to your heart, Hanne. Think of Mem Pockets and the farm. May the Seven Sister Stars grant that your choice be true."

Hanne hopped to the edge of the deep hole. Her heart pounded louder than the sea. The little hen peered down. Without hesitating, she dropped to its bottom. The moon's light made the grains of sand sparkle and shimmer. Hanne turned her head from side to side and studied all the grains.

Please, Sister Stars, she prayed. Let me choose the three grains that will help me save the farm and Mem Pockets.

As Hanne stared at the countless grains of sand, she saw three grains that looked like three tiny eggs nestled in the sand. Hanne stretched her neck forward and ate the three grains. She scrambled out of the hole and shook the sand from her feathers.

"Thank you . . . ," she began. But the ancient sea turtle was gone. Hanne could see only his trail carved into the sand that led back into the sea. Overhead the full moon shone brightly. The Seven Sister Stars twinkled, and then faded from sight.

Hanne stood and listened to the sea. She had eaten all nine grains.

The little hen shook her feathers once again. She stretched her legs and spread her toes wide in the soft sand. Hanne breathed in deeply the salty air.

"Oyster shells," she said to the night sky. "I love oyster shells."

She felt a very different hen than she was when she had first set out from the farm on her quest.

Hanne knew without any doubt that she would save Mem Pockets and her beloved farm.

But at that moment, the little hen was tired and wanted only to sleep. By the light of the full moon she set off to find a safe place to roost, far from the pounding sea.

Chapter Six

TO MARKET

HANNE AWOKE BEFORE dawn the next morning. For the first time in many days she felt rested and refreshed. The little hen was eager to begin her journey home. More than anything else she longed to see Mem Pockets, the farm, and her friends.

Hanne now knew why the crushed oyster shells that Mem Pockets fed the hens had such a salty taste—they came from the sea!

"Wait till I tell the hens," she said to herself. "They will be amazed."

It had taken Hanne two weeks to reach the sea. The little hen knew that the moon would begin to wane; its monthly cycle was halfway finished. She had to get back to the farm in time to lay the three golden eggs that would help Mem Pockets save the farm.

How in the world will I be able to lay three golden eggs? Hanne wondered.

She did not feel any more magical than when she had first set off on her journey. Would the nine grains that she had eaten truly make it possible for her to lay the golden eggs?

In her head she heard Pieter's voice.

We cannot choose our Fate in this world. We can only do our best and get on with it.

"I shall get on with it," said Hanne. She knew that Pieter was right.

The mole's words boosted Hanne's courage. She truly believed that she would lay the three golden eggs. The farm would be saved.

Hanne quickly began walking east, away from the sea. She felt happier than she had in a long time. Her scaly feet seemed to barely touch the ground as she scurried through the grass, over stones, and along well-worn paths.

As she trekked homeward, her thoughts turned to the words the Atecotti had spoken.

Each of these grains holds great magic that we have bestowed upon them. Their power and magic comes from the stones themselves and will grant your wish that you are able to fulfill your quest.

How strange that so many powerful figures took such interest in one small hen's quest, she thought.

Hanne trotted as quickly as her legs would go.

"If only there was a faster way," she said aloud.

Again she thought of the seabirds and their effortless flight on the winds.

"But a hen cannot soar the way seabirds do." Hanne sighed.

By early morning Hanne had reached the banks of a busy canal. Brightly colored boats were tied to the sides of the canal. There were many ducks paddling in the water. The little hen watched the activity around the canal. Presently, a boy came out of a house on the opposite side of the canal from where she stood. The boy looked familiar.

The boy began loading sacks into a small red boat. He dragged a heavy sack to the edge of the canal and lowered it carefully into the boat.

"That boy is going to the Market," Hanne said to herself. "Perhaps it is the Market where Mem Pockets goes every Friday."

Suddenly, an idea came to the little hen, and she knew that she must act quickly if her plan was to work.

Hanne ran to the edge of the canal where the ducks were swimming and nibbling the weeds that grew in the water. "Excuse me," Hanne called to the ducks.

The ducks swam closer to where she stood on the bank of the canal. "Do you know that boy who is putting the sacks into the boat?"

The ducks gazed up at Hanne with their bright, beady eyes. Their yellow bills opened and closed, and they all began chattering and quacking at once. Hanne could not understand a single word of their nasal speech.

"Please, please," she cried. "Only one at a time. I cannot listen to you all if you speak at the same time."

A spotted brown duck rose up on her feet out of the water, flapped her wings, and called for silence.

"I will speak to the hen," she said. "Goot morning, madam. And how are you today? It is a loverly day to be out for a walking, isn't it?"

Hanne nodded her head vigorously in reply to the duck's comments. She wished the duck would answer the one important question as to who the boy was who was loading the red boat. But Hanne knew that it would be no use to try to hurry a duck. Ducks liked to ramble and insisted on polite conversation even if the conversation had no point.

"Good morning to you all," said Hanne. "It is a lovely day. I wish you all could come for a walk with me. But I am in rather a hurry, and that's why I asked about the boy."

Hanne glanced over and saw that the boy was nearly finished loading the boat. She knew that he would be ready to leave very soon.

Hanne turned back to the duck that had spoken to her.

"Please, can you tell me if today is Friday?" asked Hanne eagerly. "And is that boy going to the Market where they sell eggs, dog biscuits, and crushed oyster shells?"

"Well, madam," said the duck. "Today is Friday, and will be all day. The boy there is young Oother. A very pleasant young boy, I must say. He is on his way to the Market in Skara Bree. It is the only Market that I know of. Master Oother takes his vegetables and oyster shells to sell there every Friday and brings back tasty corn for us."

Oother? thought Hanne. I know that name.

"Oh, thank you!" cried Hanne. "This is wonderful news. My mistress goes to the Market in Skara Bree every Friday also. If I can get there quickly, I may be able to find her, and she will take me back to our farm."

The ducks began speaking and quacking all at once. This news excited them greatly.

"So far from home," said a fat duck.

"And all alone, too," said a white duck.

"One small hen," said a long-necked gray duck. "Who would have thought!"

And so their comments went.

"Quiet, please," said Hanne in her loudest voice. "I need to ask one last very important question."

The ducks became silent at once.

"Will the boy, Oother, take me in his boat to the Market?"

"Well, madam," said the brown duck. "Our Oother is as fine a boy as they come. I am certain he would not mind one small passenger such as yourself. Look, he is getting ready to leave now."

Hanne saw Oother untying the ropes that secured his boat.

"I must get to the other side of the canal," said Hanne.

"The bridge," quacked the ducks in unison. "Run to the bridge!"

"Thank you!" cried Hanne. "Thank you for all your help."

Hanne ran as fast as she could to the bridge. Oother's boat was slowly moving out into the middle of the canal. Hanne reached the bridge and gasped for breath. She watched as the little boat came closer. Oother paddled the boat carefully and steadily. He did not see the little black speckled hen standing on the bridge. Hanne had to act quickly.

As the boat began to glide under the bridge, the little hen jumped.

Oother ducked his head as the boat passed under the bridge. He did not see the little hen leap off the bridge, wings flapping, and land with a THUMP! onto his sack of oyster shells.

Hanne sat stunned on the sack. She knew that if she had missed the boat, she would have plunged into the canal. Unlike ducks, she could not swim. Her experience in the sea had been enough for her.

Oother raised his head and saw a little black speckled hen sitting quietly on the sack of oyster shells. The boy laughed out loud.

"Hallo, there," he said. "Where did ye come from?"

He scratched his head and looked back toward the bridge.

"Nay, it was no' possible . . ." But his words trailed off.

Oother stared at Hanne and the little hen stared back. She cocked her head to one side. Her bright yellow eyes looked the boy up and down. Oother knew he was being carefully considered.

"I've seen ye before somewheres," said Oother. "Ye look very familiar."

Hanne said nothing.

Oother removed his cap.

A wee black speckled hen, he thought to himself. Noo where have I seen speckled hens?

Oother put his cap back on and smiled at Hanne.

"Ye're wanting to go to Market, eh?" he said as he easily paddled the boat down the canal.

Hanne cocked her head to the other side.

"Well, I cannot turn back noo," said the boy. "Ye'll have t' come along wi' me and behave yerself. I will bring ye back at the end of the day and try to find out who ye belong to. I keen that I've seen ye hereaboots somewhere."

Hanne was thrilled! She was going to Market. She would find Mem Pockets and everything would be well.

It was exciting being on a boat. Hanne liked the gentle rocking motion that almost lulled her to sleep. She watched the changing scenery on either side of the canal. Oother chattered away, just the way Mem Pockets did, as if he knew the hen could understand every word he said. And he sang boat songs!

Hanne liked the sound of his voice. The boy sang beautifully.

Proud, elegant swans dipped their heads as the boat passed by. Oother and Hanne passed many old stone houses built alongside the canal. Thick, green mosses grew at the base of the houses where the walls touched the water. Oother steered the boat under low bridges and sometimes through the branches of willows overhanging the canal.

Hanne loved the canal.

In the distance Hanne saw a cluster of stone buildings. Some of the buildings had tiled red roofs. Others were thatched with yellow straw. She had never seen so many buildings tightly packed together, nor so many canals. Skara Bree was a village of canals.

Oother knew his way by heart through the crisscrossing maze of canals and stone bridges. People called to him from above, "Hallo, Oother! Who is your new passenger, eh?"

Hanne turned this way and that, hoping not to miss any of the excitement that buzzed everywhere. When she looked up, she could see only steep stone walls and windowpanes glinting in the bright morning light. Pigeons flew low over the canal, nearly skimming its surface with their wings.

Oother eased the boat alongside a small landing. Stone steps led up from the canal to the street.

"Noo listen," he said to Hanne. "Ye're goin' t' have t' behave yerself and stick close by me or else ye'll get lost. And then there is no tellin' what will happen t' ye."

The speckled hen sat still and listened carefully to his words. Oother loved animals and birds and trusted them to have a bit of sense about them. Hanne instinctively trusted the boy.

Oother quickly unloaded his sacks of vegetables and oyster shells and carried them one by one up the stone steps. Hanne remained on the boat. After the last sack had been carried up to the street, Oother returned to the boat.

"Come on, then," he said to Hanne. "I have t' get t' my stand."

He picked up the little hen and placed her on his shoulder. Hanne gripped his shoulder tightly and held on.

Oother had placed the sacks in a wooden cart. He wheeled the cart expertly through the crowded street. Hanne saw people everywhere. She saw baskets of flowers, hanging bunches of braided onions, huge wooden barrels, and many other wondrous sights. She smelled the delicious aroma of fresh baked bread and buns. There was an air of excitement everywhere.

And the noise! Hanne had thought the henwoodie sometimes was noisy, but in the village the noise was unbelievable.

Oother stopped in front of an empty stand. He set down the cart and brushed off his hands.

"Here we be," he said.

He took Hanne from his shoulder and placed her on the wooden table.

"Stay there while I unpack m' vegetables," Oother told the hen.

Hanne did not dare move. She stayed where he put her and watched the passersby. Hanne hoped to see Mem Pockets. Soon Oother had unpacked all the vegetables. He opened the sack of oyster shells and set it in front of the stand. He stuck a large wooden scoop in the oyster shells so that he could measure out how much someone might want to buy.

Hanne breathed in the salty sea smell and remembered Old Murdaugh.

Hanne watched with great interest as people came and inspected Oother's vegetables.

"Beautiful carrots, Oother," said an old woman wearing a dark dress and hat. She bought the carrots and placed them in her basket.

"No finer cabbages to be found anywhere," said a man as he paid Oother for three large heads of cabbage.

Several people offered to buy the little black hen, but Oother always told them that she was not for sale.

The day wore on, and by midafternoon Hanne began to worry. She would never find Mem Pockets if she remained in one place. She would have to search the entire Market if she was ever to find her mistress. But the Market was enormous!

As Hanne sat and thought what to do, a familiar hat came into view. It was a wide-brimmed green hat with a faded red ribbon wrapped around it. Hanne recognized the hat immediately. It was Mem Pockets!

Chapter Seven

THE SLY FOX

HANNE CLUCKED LOUDLY to Mem Pockets, causing Oother to drop the vegetables he was holding. Mem Pockets's hat disappeared into the crowd. The little hen had to act quickly.

Hanne jumped off the table and darted into the tangle of legs and feet. She ran as fast as she could toward the spot where she had seen Mem Pockets. Oother called out to her to come back, but he could not leave his stand to chase after her. The boy shook his head sadly and sighed.

Maybe she knows where she's going, he thought.

Hanne found herself scrambling among an impassable throng of legs and feet. Long skirts and cloaks blocked her view. She was nearly stepped on repeatedly. The little hen struggled to keep her wits about her. She dodged through the legs and flapped her way through the Market.

Where had Mem Pockets gone?

Hanne had not realized that the Market would be so crowded with people. She had felt certain that when she saw Mem Pockets, she could simply run to her mistress and be taken back to the farm. She now found herself in a situation more terrifying than any she had been in before.

For an hour or more Hanne fought her way through the maze of legs. She saw a stone bridge crossing a canal and dashed toward it as quickly as she could. Hanne ran across the bridge and found herself in a paved courtyard. The courtyard was empty.

Hanne looked around but saw no one.

Suddenly she was grabbed from behind and held high in the air.

"Well, noo," said a gruff voice. "Ain't thoo a loverly wee hen."

A man with a thick, black, bristling beard held Hanne upside down by her feet. He smiled broadly at her.

"Ye'll fit jes' perfect in me pot back home," he said.

The man tucked the little hen under his arm and sauntered down a narrow street.

Hanne could not think. It had all happened so quickly. The man whistled as he ambled through the village. He kept a firm grip on Hanne under one arm and carried a large basket filled with his purchases in the other.

Hanne looked desperately around. She struggled to get away, but the man only gripped her tighter, squeezing the breath out of her.

It is the foolish hen who is caught by the sly fox, said a voice.

I have been foolish, thought Hanne bitterly. I did not keep my wits about

me. Now I will never find Mem Pockets or see the farm again.

Hanne's heart ached. She squeezed her eyes shut and tried to think what to do. She must find Mem Pockets. The predicament in which she found herself seemed hopeless.

The man pressed Hanne tighter under his arm and thumped her on the head. Hanne pecked hard at the man's hand.

"I was not drowned by the sea," Hanne said to herself. "And I will not be taken by this sly fox!"

As Hanne gathered her strength for one final attempt at freedom, she heard a familiar voice cry out.

"Hanne! Hanne!"

It was Mem Pockets! Hanne's eyes flew open, and she saw Mem Pockets rushing toward her, followed by Daisy, who was barking loudly.

Hanne could not believe that Mem Pockets had found her. Then she heard Old Murdaugh's voice in her head.

It is the Knowing of the Names. You called to your Mistress by thinking her name. In her heart she heard you. It is one of the Great Mysteries.

I wonder *how*, thought Hanne.

Hanne was overjoyed to see the old woman and dog. She squirmed more frantically under the man's arm. His grip on her loosened, she flew from his arms, and she ran straight to Mem Pockets.

Mem Pockets scooped her from the ground and held her tenderly. Tears rolled down her cheeks as she held the little hen.

"Hanne, oh, Hanne. I thought you were lost forever."

"Oy," said the man with the black beard. "Oy, that's me hen ye got there."

"I beg your pardon," said Mem Pockets.

"That's me hen," said the man angrily.

"She is *my* hen," said Mem Pockets.

A crowd had gathered to watch the argument. Hanne ruffed out her feathers and glared at the man indignantly.

"I said, that's me hen. Give 'er back to me."

The man tried to snatch Hanne from Mem Pockets.

"I will not give her back," said Mem Pockets calmly. "She belongs to me."

Hanne shivered in Mem Pockets's arms. Could this sly fox take her from her mistress? How could she prove that she belonged to Mem Pockets?

A red-bearded constable appeared.

"QUIET!" he shouted. "All right, what's going on here?"

Everyone began speaking at once. To Hanne they sounded just like the ducks on the canal.

"She took me hen," said the man, pointing his finger at Mem Pockets. "And I want 'er back. She's goin' t' be me family's dinner tonight."

Hanne's heart nearly stopped.

"She is *not* your hen," said Mem Pockets. "Her name is Hanne. I don't know how you came to have her, but she has been missing from my farm for more than two weeks. I have been searching everywhere for her."

Mem Pockets stroked Hanne's head. The little hen felt calmer.

An old man stepped out of the crowd.

"That's right," he said. "That hen belongs to Mem Pockets the Egg Lady.

She is the only one around these parts who keeps speckled hens. And she has been selling her eggs in this Market since I was a young man."

"Says yerself," said the man who had snatched Hanne in the courtyard. "I need more proof than yer word that this scrawny little hen belongs to that old fishwife."

"I can prove that she is my hen," said Mem Pockets. "I have something here that might convince you that she belongs to me."

Mem Pockets rummaged in her basket and took out a small bundle wrapped in a handkerchief. She unwrapped the bundle and held up the last speckled egg.

"See," said the old man. "Her hens are the only hens that have speckles on their back like the speckles on that egg."

"That's true," said a woman in the crowd. "I always buy my eggs from Mem Pockets."

"I'd recognize her eggs anywhere," said a woman holding a baby.

"Me, too," said a boy's voice.

It was Oother. He had left his stand to try to find Hanne.

"Mem Pockets always buys a sack of crushed oyster shells from me for her Scaldy hens," he said. "I deliver the sack to her farm because it's too heavy for her to carry home by herself. And I've seen that hen on her farm, scratching aboot in the gardens."

"YOU, sir, have some explaining to do," said the constable.

He took the man with the black, bristling beard by the arm and led him off down the street.

The crowd cheered and congratulated Mem Pockets on finding her lost hen.

"Thank you, Oother," said Mem Pockets. "If you hadn't spoken up, I'm not certain my egg would have convinced the constable that Hanne belonged to me."

Oother grinned broadly.

"Mem Pockets, ye won't believe what happened this morning when I was settin' off t' come t' Market."

And he told her the story of how Hanne had dropped into his boat miles away from Skara Bree.

"Hanne," said Mem Pockets. "You are a brave hen. Where in the world have you been all this time? You feel so thin. I must get you home where you belong. Although it will not be our home much longer."

"Thank you again, Oother," said Mem Pockets. "Please, take this egg and buy yourself some babblers."

The boy protested, but the old woman insisted that he take the egg.

"Thank you," Oother said. "I do love babblers."

"Will you bring the sack of oyster shells to the farm a bit later?"

Oother smiled and nodded his head. He tipped his hat to Mem Pockets, winked at Hanne, and strode back to his stand.

I am going home at last, thought Hanne. I am tired of adventures. I want to see the hens and be back on the farm.

Mem Pockets placed Hanne in her basket and walked back to the farm. Daisy sniffed at the little hen and wagged her tail.

Chapter Eight

RETURNING HOME

HANNE FELT SAFE and happy sitting in Mem Pockets's basket. The basket bounced gently as the old woman walked briskly down the road. Mem Pockets kept glancing in the basket to make sure Hanne was really there. Daisy kept a close eye on the basket as well.

It was a crisp autumn day—Friday, all day, as the brown duck had said. Hanne clucked softly to herself. She had always loved Market Day. And she had been to the Market!

Wait till I tell the other hens about the Market, she thought to herself.

Late in the afternoon Mem Pockets, Hanne, and Daisy reached the farm. Hanne stared wide-eyed at the familiar stone buildings. She breathed deeply the wonderful smells of the farm that she had missed so much.

"Hallo," called a voice behind them.

Mem Pockets, Hanne, and Daisy turned at the sound. Mem Pockets smiled.

It was Oother. He had brought the sack of crushed oyster shells and was ready to make his own journey home.

"Thank you, Oother," said Mem Pockets. "Wait a minute. I have a wee something for you."

"Och, no, Mem Pockets," the boy said. "Ye don't have t' give me anything. The egg was enough. I was happy t' bring the sack of oyster shells t' you."

Mem Pockets smiled more broadly and shook her head. She pulled a bar of dark chocolate from one of her many pockets.

"For the journey home," she said.

Oother smiled.

"Thanks," he said. "That's my favorite chocolate." He winked at Hanne and strolled off down the road, singing.

Mem Pockets walked straight to the house.

"Hanne, you need food and you must be kept warm," she said. "I will take you back to the henwoodie in the morning."

Hanne was thrilled!

Mem Pockets set the basket on the table. She lifted Hanne from the basket and inspected her carefully. She examined each of Hanne's wings to make certain nothing was broken.

"Only a few feathers roughed up a bit," she said. "That awful man!"

She gently pressed each foot to see if Hanne felt any soreness.

"You seem to be all in one piece," said Mem Pockets, smiling. "A bit thinner, but all in one piece."

The kitchen was warm and smelled of fresh baked bread. It had a scrubbed stone floor, tall wooden cupboards, and a large stone fireplace where a black iron kettle hung over the fire, softly hissing. In the center of the kitchen was an old oak table that had been in Mem Pockets's family for more than two hundred years. There were several straw-backed chairs and wooden benches around the table. Mem Pockets was fond of visitors.

In one corner was a round beehive oven where Mem Pockets baked her bread. The newly baked bread sat on a stone shelf set into the wall. Beautiful lace curtains hung at the windows. Hanne knew that Mem Pockets's mother and grandmother had been lace-makers. The lace curtains were light and airy. Hanne could see through them to the farmyard outside.

Mem Pockets hugged Hanne to her.

"Don't ever leave this farm again," she said. "We missed you very much."

Mem Pockets took the evening meal out to the animals in the barn. She walked to the henwoodie, greeted the hens, and gave them their evening meal and their special treat of crushed oyster shells.

"Eat well, my darlings," Mem Pockets said. "Tomorrow I have a surprise for you."

And she sang them a beautiful egg-laying song.

"Good night, my dears," she said cheerfully. "We shall see you in the morning."

After Mem Pockets had closed the door, the hens stopped eating and chattering. They were puzzled. Ever since Hanne had left, Mem Pockets had been very quiet. She always looked tired and sad. Tonight the old woman had bustled

about the henwoodie. She had given the hens extra feed and their favorite treat of crushed oyster shells. And she had promised another surprise the next day.

The hens could not imagine what had come over their mistress.

"Perhaps she found some money," said Rose Madder.

"Maybe she's getting married," said Pyn, the most romantic hen the henwoodie had ever housed.

"Or perhaps," said Gemma, "she's not going to lose the farm after all."

"We shall have to wait until morning," said Old Pegotty. "And then we shall see what we shall see."

The old hen smiled to herself.

Hanne spent a peaceful night in the kitchen. The kitchen was the warmest room in the old house. A warm glow dimly lit the room. Both Mem Pockets and Daisy stayed there with her. Mem Pockets would not let the little hen out of her sight. She and Daisy would watch her all through the night.

Hanne loved the old woman more than ever. She was glad that she had gone to the barrow. She had been thrilled to meet the Atecotti. She had survived the Great Green Sea. And she had met Old Murdaugh.

Now she was back on the farm. For the first time in many days, Hanne slept soundly.

Chapter Nine

THREE GOLDEN EGGS

IN THE MORNING Mem Pockets picked up Hanne and marched to the henwoodie. Daisy followed, barking happily.

The old woman threw open the door to the henwoodie. "Look who is back, my darlings!" she cried.

The hens stared at Mem Pockets. Had the old woman lost her mind? Then they saw Hanne. The hens began clucking and cackling at once. They rushed to the old woman, craning their necks to get a better view of the little black hen.

Mem Pockets fussed and fretted with Hanne and placed her in her favorite spot on the roost. The old woman tipped a large scoop of feed into the trough and gazed at her hens with pride.

"You are all my fabulous speckled hens," she said.

After she had made certain everything was in order, Mem Pockets opened the door.

"I will be back shortly, my dears," she said. "I know you all have a great deal to talk about."

She closed the door and walked back to the house.

After Mem Pockets had gone, Hanne hopped down from the roost. The hens gathered around her.

"Hanne," they cried. "We are so glad to have you back."

"Last night Mem Pockets told us she had a surprise for us, but we had no idea it was you!" said Sophie.

"Welcome home, Hanne!" said Rose Madder and Pyn.

"Oh, Hanne," said Gemma and Maille. "Welcome home."

The hens clucked and fussed over the little hen. No one dared ask the one question they all wanted to ask: Had Hanne succeeded in her quest?

At last, Old Pegotty cleared her throat.

"Hush now," she said. "Let Hanne breathe. You have not given her a moment's peace since her return."

The old hen waddled over to Hanne and stared at her closely.

"Welcome home, Hanne," she said. "You have been in our thoughts every day since you left. We have fretted and worried about your safety every night. We are truly happy to have you back home."

"Thank you," said Hanne. "It is wonderful to be back. I have so much to tell you all." The hens pressed closer, eager to hear Hanne's story.

"I did go to the barrow. I met the most interesting little mole who is the Keeper of the Barrow," said Hanne. "I went to the Standing Stones, and they changed into the Atecotti—the Keepers of the Stones. And I reached the Great Green Sea!"

As she said this, Hanne shuddered at the memory of being in the icy sea. "I did my best and now I'm back."

Throughout the morning Hanne recounted to the flock of hens the details of her adventures. The hens gasped when she told them about the moaning barrow-wight in the pitch blackness of the barrow. They clucked and shook their wattles when she described the mysterious Atecotti. The hens were awestruck when she told them about the icy cold sea and about being rescued by the God of the Sea.

Hanne did not reveal his name to them.

"You are the bravest hen!" cried Gemma.

"And the purest, too," said Pyn. "Hanne, none of us could have done what you have done."

"And," said Old Pegotty quietly, "she is the wisest hen. Hanne, you kept your wits about you, and you have done your task well. We are all proud of you."

Again, the old hen looked closely at Hanne. She seemed to be looking for something.

"Hanne," she said quietly. "There is not much time left. Do you think you will be able to lay the golden eggs?"

The hens were silent. At last the question had been asked that was foremost in all their minds. Would Hanne be able to complete her quest and lay the golden eggs?

Hanne lifted her head and gazed at the hens. She looked at each one in turn and knew in her heart that each hen had prayed for her success. Hanne looked into Old Pegotty's eyes.

"Yes, I shall lay the golden eggs that will save the farm."

The hens began talking at once.

"There is so much to do," said Rose Madder.

"Hanne, you must have the most comfortable nesting cubby," said Gemma.

"You must sit in the warmest place," said Pyn.

"You must eat the most grain," said Sophie.

"You must drink lots of water," said Maille.

"You must just be yourself," said Old Pegotty.

"My own nesting cubby is just fine, thank you," said Hanne quietly. "I don't need anything special to lay the golden eggs."

In her heart there was no doubt.

That afternoon the hens left Hanne to herself. Mem Pockets let the hens out of the henwoodie to scratch in the farmyard. They pecked and clucked excitedly, but none of the hens strayed too far from the henwoodie in case Hanne should need them.

Late in the afternoon the hens returned to the henwoodie. Quietly, they tiptoed to Hanne's nesting cubby. The little hen sat still, hardly breathing. She stared straight ahead. Her face had a blank expression.

"Oh, Hanne," cried Maille. "You didn't lay a golden egg!"

The hens began to cackle. They clucked and fussed around the little hen. They preened her feathers and gently pecked her head.

Hanne sat and stared. And stared.

"Hanne," said Old Pegotty in a hushed voice. "You must tell us. Did you lay a golden egg?"

Hanne looked blankly at the old hen as if she did not understand.

Hanne slowly stood up in the nest. The hens pressed closer to see what she had laid. In the straw was a golden egg—a perfect, shining golden egg.

Everyone spoke at once.

"She did it!" cried Pyn.

"She laid a golden egg!" clucked Rose Madder.

"Hanne, you are marvelous!" said Maille.

"Mem Pockets and the farm are saved!" said Gemma.

"And so are we," said Sophie.

"Wait," said Old Pegotty. "We must not let Mem Pockets know about the egg until all three eggs have been laid. Then Hanne will present the eggs to her. We shall have to wait and see what happens."

The hens agreed that this was the sensible and wise thing to do. Hanne hid the golden egg under the straw in her nest. She felt light-headed and weak. Laying the golden egg had drained her of most of her strength. Old Pegotty gazed at the little hen closely.

"Hanne," she said. "Are you all right?"

"Yes," said Hanne.

Old Pegotty looked hard at the little hen, then walked to her own nesting cubby, deep in thought.

The next day Hanne stayed in her nesting cubby. She felt too weak to move. The hens brought her food, a mouthful at a time. Their closeness cheered the little hen, and she was glad of their company. Mem Pockets stroked her head and sang soft songs to her.

"Just rest, Hanne," the old woman said.

But Hanne could not lay another golden egg.

It was three days later that Hanne laid the second golden egg. And three days after that, she laid the third. Three golden eggs lay in the straw in her nest.

Hanne looked spent and frail.

"Hanne, your task is done," said Old Pegotty. "Now you must rest."

The old hen nuzzled Hanne's neck, the way she used to do when Hanne was a chick. She loved the little black hen and knew that laying the three golden eggs had cost Hanne dearly.

That afternoon Mem Pockets came into the henwoodie as usual.

"Good afternoon, my darlings," she said softly.

The hens did not cluck or cackle. They were unusually silent.

"Tomorrow the money must be paid for the farm taxes. I'm afraid I still do not have it. We are going to lose the farm after all."

The old woman wiped the tears from her eyes and fussed with her apron.

"I am so sorry, my dears."

The hens clustered around her feet. They pecked eagerly at her clogs and tugged on her apron. The hens tried to lead Mem Pockets to Hanne's nesting cubby.

"Oh, dear," cried Mem Pockets. "Is something wrong? Where's Hanne?"

The old woman looked wildly around the henwoodie and saw Hanne sitting quietly in her own nesting cubby. Alone. Mem Pockets went to the little hen and saw that she did not look well.

Hanne's eyes were dull; their brightness was gone. Her sleek black feathers

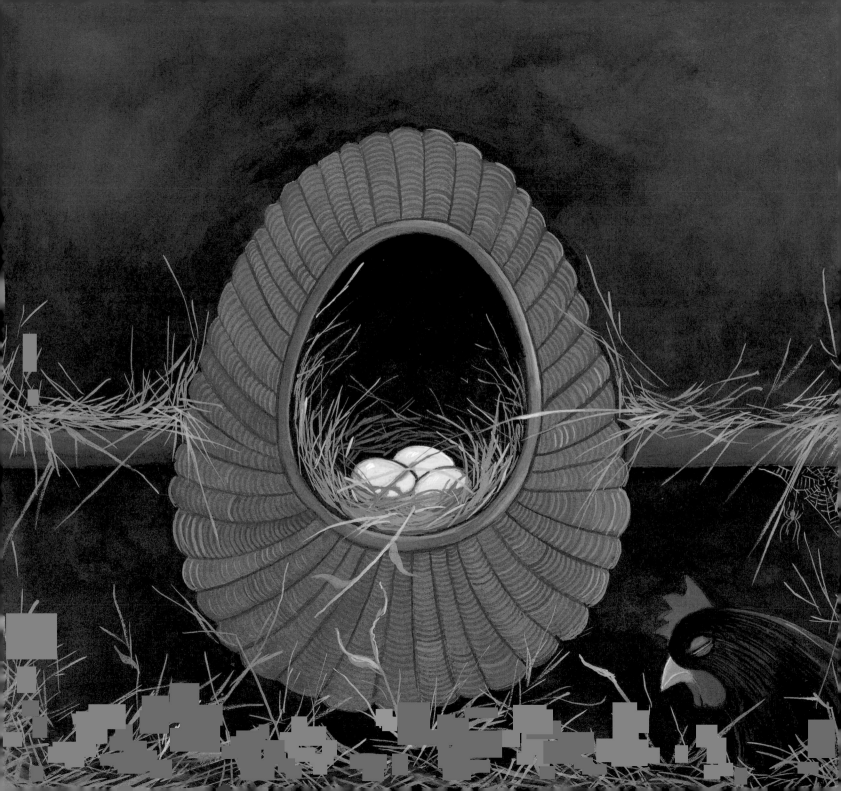

had lost their sheen. Her nesting cubby was littered with tattered feathers that had fallen out.

"Oh, Hanne!" cried Mem Pockets. "Whatever is the matter?"

Mem Pockets lifted Hanne from the nest and held her tenderly in her arms. She stroked the hen's head and held her close to her heart. Mem Pockets saw something glittering in the straw in Hanne's nest.

She stared into Hanne's nest and saw three golden eggs.

Mem Pockets looked from the eggs to Hanne and back to the eggs again. She could not believe her eyes. Hens did not lay golden eggs. But Hanne had.

"I . . . I don't believe it," the old woman stammered.

The hens began cackling and clucking all at once. They were excited.

Mem Pockets placed the golden eggs in her egg basket.

"I'll be back, my dears," she said.

Mem Pockets carried Hanne to the house.

The hens all talked at once. Only Old Pegotty seemed worried.

"I do not think Hanne will live," she said quietly.

The hens fell silent.

In the kitchen, Mem Pockets carefully placed Hanne in a basket. She wrapped a soft shawl around the little hen and tucked it in.

"Hanne, you must stay here where it is warm," said Mem Pockets.

The old woman stirred up the fire and added more wood. She heated milk in a pot and stirred finely ground oats into it. When the porridge was ready, Mem Pockets spooned it into Hanne's beak. She gently stroked Hanne's throat until the hen swallowed the warm food.

After Hanne had swallowed as much of the porridge as she could, she closed her eyes, and her head dropped onto her breast.

Mem Pockets took Hanne out of the basket, tucked the shawl tightly around the little hen, and held her against her heart. Hanne was weak, and Mem Pockets feared that she would die.

Hanne slipped into a fitful sleep.

In her dreams she saw the barrow and Pieter. The little mole was telling her something, but she could not hear what he said. Then, as if from very far away, she heard his tiny voice.

Oh, miss, you must do the best you can.

Swirling mists clouded the dream. Out of the mists rose three gray standing stones. Hanne stared at the stones and watched as they slowly changed into the Atecotti. The Atecotti looked at her sadly. Hanne heard Grainne's soft voice chanting.

In the Standing Stones great power is kept. This power comes from the earth and is a gift from the Goddess herself. Dream your wish, brave Hanne. Your wish has been granted. Be at peace, little one. Your time has not yet come.

Hanne shuddered in Mem Pockets's arms. The old woman choked back her sobs. Hanne was slipping away. A single tear fell from the old woman's eye and landed on Hanne's beak.

In her dreams, Hanne smelled the salt sea. She heard the raucous seabirds crying overhead. She longed to soar with them. Hanne heard the roar of the sea on sand. And in her dreams she soared with the birds. Her body was light as air, and flying was effortless.

Hanne heard Old Murdaugh's deep voice speaking to her.

Wisdom begins with the knowledge that there is much to learn. Great wisdom lies in the Knowing of Names. Listen, small one, listen . . . the Magic is in your name.

Hanne soared on and on until her wings began to tire. Slowly, as if time held her back, she began tumbling toward the sea. She shivered as she remembered how icy cold the sea was. Cold as death.

"Hanne," called a voice from very far away. "Hanne, oh, Hanne."

The little hen could no longer hear the sea. She could only hear her name being called over and over. In her dream the Seven Sister Stars shone brightly.

Not yet, they said. And the stars faded into the blackness.

Hanne's head jerked up.

"Oh, Hanne!" cried Mem Pockets. "Hanne, oh, Hanne."

Mem Pockets held the hen tightly against her face. Her tears soaked Hanne's feathers. The tears tasted salty. As Mem Pockets held Hanne close, she felt the hen's heart beat a little stronger. Hanne opened her eyes. They were no longer dull and clouded.

The little hen gazed at the snug kitchen, listened to the steaming kettle, and felt the old woman's heart beating hard against her breast.

Mem Pockets stayed awake all night, holding the little hen and singing to her. Mem Pockets did not sing as beautifully as the boy, Oother. But to Hanne, it was the most beautiful voice in the world.

In the morning, Hanne ate everything Mem Pockets fed her. She was ravenous! Hanne preened her feathers and stretched her legs. Mem Pockets clucked and fussed over her and made certain she was comfortable.

"Hanne," said Mem Pockets. "You are the bravest little hen I have ever known." The old woman gazed at the speckled hen.

"But, Hanne," she said, "the farm is not worth your life. I want you to know that."

Hanne cocked her head and playfully pecked Mem Pockets's hand.

"I don't know how you did it. But the golden eggs will save the farm. I think you may have saved the farm for several lifetimes!"

That afternoon Mem Pockets took two of the golden eggs into the village. She paid the outstanding owed farm taxes on the farm. There was enough money left over to put away for a long, long time.

Mem Pockets found Oother's stand and bought fresh vegetables and a sack of crushed oyster shells from the boy. She gave him a gold coin.

"For luck," she said.

Oother smiled and hugged the old woman.

Mem Pockets went to Hobson's Sweets Shop and bought ten pounds of babblers. Now she could suck them with her coffee anytime she wanted. She bought baked biscuits for Daisy. She filled her pockets with kernels of corn. She bought as much dark chocolate as her pockets would hold.

As she walked through the village, she handed out the chocolate to every child she met. She gave every dog a biscuit. She scattered handfuls of corn to the birds and pigeons.

Then the old woman walked home with Daisy trotting by her side.

When she reached the farm, she went to the henwoodie.

"Hello, my darlings," she sang. "I'm back."

The hens clustered around the old woman's feet, pecking at her clogs.

Mem Pockets held up the third golden egg that she had not taken into the village. "This will be our nest egg," she said.

"Just in case we ever need money again."

In the spring Hanne and the hens each laid a clutch of eggs. Each hen sat on her eggs and brooded for twenty-one days. Mem Pockets kept a close watch over the hens to make certain no sly foxes hurt them. Spring flowers burst into bloom. When the eggs hatched, cheeping speckled peepers overran the farm.

Mem Pockets was happy to see all the new chicks. She let them scratch in the gardens, and she sang them growing songs.

Every morning Hanne brought her brood into the kitchen and showed them where Mem Pockets baked her delicious brown bread.

The little black speckled hen never laid another golden egg.

Patricia Lee Gauch, Editor

PHILOMEL BOOKS
A division of Penguin Young Readers Group.   Published by The Penguin Group.
Penguin Group (USA) Inc., 375 Hudson Street, New York, NY 10014, U.S.A.
Penguin Group (Canada), 90 Eglinton Avenue East, Suite 700, Toronto, Ontario, Canada M4P 2Y3 (a division of Pearson Penguin Canada Inc.)
Penguin Books Ltd, 80 Strand, London WC2R 0RL, England.
Penguin Ireland, 25 St. Stephen's Green, Dublin 2, Ireland (a division of Penguin Books Ltd).
Penguin Group (Australia), 250 Camberwell Road, Camberwell, Victoria 3124, Australia (a division of Pearson Australia Group Pty Ltd).
Penguin Books India Pvt Ltd, 11 Community Centre, Panchsheel Park, New Delhi - 110 017, India.
Penguin Group (NZ), Cnr Airborne and Rosedale Roads, Albany, Auckland 1310, New Zealand (a division of Pearson New Zealand Ltd).
Penguin Books (South Africa) (Pty) Ltd, 24 Sturdee Avenue, Rosebank, Johannesburg 2196, South Africa.
Penguin Books Ltd, Registered Offices: 80 Strand, London WC2R 0RL, England.

Manufactured in China by South China Printing Co. Ltd.   Design by Semadar Megged.
The artwork is rendered in gouache on 140 lb. d'Arches rough watercolour paper.
Library of Congress Cataloging-in-Publication Data
Dunrea, Olivier.   Hanne's quest / Olivier Dunrea.   p. cm.   Summary: On an island off the coast of Scotland, a young hen must prove herself pure, wise, and brave in a quest to help her beloved owner, Mem Pockets, from losing her family's farm. [1. Fairy tales. 2. Chickens—Fiction. 3. Voyages and travels—Fiction. 4. Farm life—Scotland—Fiction. 5. Orkney (Scotland)—Fiction. 6. Scotland—Fiction.] I. Title.
PZ8.D965Han 2006   [Fic]—dc22   2004009091
ISBN 0-399-24216-3
1 3 5 7 9 10 8 6 4 2
First Impression